THE TWIDDLE TWINS' SINGLE FOOTPRINT MYSTERY

by HOWARD GOLDSMITH

illustrations by CHARLES JORDAN

For my late friend Tony Kallet, musician, wit, and
born teacher, whose love and deep respect for children
made each one feel special—H.G.

For Kathy, Joe, Erin, Megan, Logan, and Phalen—C.J.

Text copyright © 1998 by Howard Goldsmith
Illustrations copyright © 1998 by Charles Jordan

For information contact:
MONDO Publishing
980 Avenue of the Americas
New York, New York 10018
Visit our web site at http://www.mondopub.com

Designed by Christy Hale

Printed in the United States of America
03 04 05 06 07   9 8 7 6 5 4 3

Library of Congress Cataloging-in-Publication Data
Goldsmith, Howard.
  The Twiddle twins' single footprint mystery / by Howard Goldsmith ; illustrations by
Charles Jordan.
    p.   cm.
Summary: Tabitha and Timothy Twiddle, twin hippos, must prove to their neighbor
that they are not responsible for the mysterious footprint left in the wet cement in
front of his house.
    ISBN 1-57255-619-6 (pbk. : alk. paper)
    [1. Hippopotamus—Fiction.   2. Twins—Fiction.   3. Mystery and detective stories.]
  I. Jordan, Charles, ill.   II. Title.
PZ7.G575Tws   1998
[Fic]—dc21   98-11238
                                                                        CIP
                                                                         AC

Contents

Wet Cement

"Catch the ball!" Timothy Twiddle yelled.

Timothy threw the ball so hard it bounced right past Tabitha.

"Uh-oh!" Tabitha cried. The ball headed straight for the wet cement in front of Mr. Snipe's house.

"Yikes!" Timothy shouted.

5

Luckily, the ball hit the tape surrounding the wet cement. The ball bounced sideways and rolled to a stop.

Immediately Mr. Snipe's voice rang out. "Get away from my cement!" he shouted.

"It was an accident," Timothy answered.

"The ball didn't touch the cement," Tabitha assured Mr. Snipe.

"Next time it will," Mr. Snipe grumbled. "I've told you before—don't play ball near my house!"

"We're going to the next corner," Timothy called to Mr. Snipe. "So if anything happens to your cement, don't blame us."

"We'll be innocent," Tabitha said.

"I'll keep my eyes on you Twiddle twins," Mr. Snipe said. "I know you'd just love to write your initials in my new cement."

The twins ran to the next corner. They threw the ball back and forth.

Soon Fred Klotch came down the
street. He was swinging a stick. He
stopped in front of Mr. Snipe's house
and eyed the wet cement.

"Uh-oh!" Tabitha gasped. Fred's stick was just an inch from the cement when she screamed, "Stop!"

"Don't touch that cement!" Timothy yelled.

"Why not?" Fred asked.

"It's not your cement," Tabitha answered.

"It's not yours either," said Fred. "Why does Mr. Snipe's cement matter so much to you anyway?"

"Mr. Snipe will blame us if anything happens to it," Tabitha said. "Why don't you just go away so there won't be any problems?"

"You're two scaredy-cats," Fred teased.
"You're just afraid of Mr. Snipe."

Clarabel's ears pricked up as she
watched from a tree near Mr. Snipe's
house. She looked around for two cats.

Finally Fred decided to leave. "You can keep your dumb cement," he said.

"Bye," said the twins as they watched Fred stroll up the street.

The Footprint

The next morning, the twins ran outside to play. To their amazement, there was a footprint in the exact center of the cement.

"Why just one footprint?" Timothy wondered.

"You mean *how* just one footprint?"
Tabitha said. "How can you leave just
one footprint?"

"If you have only one foot," Timothy
said.

"I mean it," said Tabitha. "There must
be an explanation."

The twins leaned over the cement, studying the print.

"Looks like a shoe print," Tabitha said. "See the heel mark?"

"Yeah," Timothy said. "By the size, it must be someone our age."

"Fred Klotch!" they exclaimed together.

"But how come there's only one print and no other marks on the cement?" Timothy asked.

"Maybe he jumped in on one foot and out on the other," Tabitha suggested.

"Then the print would be deeper, because he'd step down hard," Timothy said.

"Someone stepped as light as a bird," Tabitha said.

"There aren't even any traces of cement on the sidewalk," Timothy said. "The cement would have stuck to his shoe and left marks on the sidewalk."

"It's a mystery," Tabitha said, shrugging her shoulders.

The twins scratched their heads, completely baffled.

Trailing Fred

Just then Fred came by, smiling from ear to ear.

"Fred looks real pleased with himself," Timothy whispered to Tabitha.

"Well, well. Look at this," Fred said to the twins. "A footprint. A *single* footprint. How do you suppose it got there?"

"You tell us," Tabitha answered. "You're so clever."

Fred laughed. "You'll have to figure that out for yourselves," he said. Then he took off down the street.

"Let's follow him," Timothy said.
"Maybe we'll find a clue."

Tabitha and Timothy followed Fred
from a distance. They ducked behind a
tree and watched him enter his house.

A garbage can stood outside the
house. Timothy looked inside. Under
some newspapers, he saw a box in a
plastic bag.

"A shoe!" Timothy exclaimed, opening
the box. "*The* shoe. The bottom is caked
with dry cement. This proves it—Fred
did it."

"Not yet," Tabitha said. She grabbed Timothy's hand and they ran to Mr. Snipe's house.

The shoe fit the print in the cement exactly.

Mr. Snipe ran out of his house. "You
two!" he shouted. "Look what you did
to my cement!"

"We didn't do it," the twins said.

"You just couldn't leave the cement alone," Mr. Snipe said. "You had to put a print in it."

"WE DIDN'T!" Tabitha cried.

"You didn't? You even have the shoe in your hands." Mr. Snipe pointed to the shoe Timothy was holding.

Timothy took a big gulp. "I-I guess I do," he said. "B-But it's not the way it looks. We can explain."

"You can explain to your parents after I tell them what happened to my new cement."

"Ugh," Tabitha groaned.

Mr. Snipe stomped inside and slammed his door.

"I guess he's mad," said Tabitha.

"I guess so," Timothy agreed.

Mismatched Shoes

That afternoon, Timothy and Tabitha saw
Fred coming out of a shoe store. He was
carrying a shoe box.

"New shoes?" Timothy asked.

"Guess you can't wear *this* shoe anymore,"
Tabitha said. "It's hard as cement."

Fred's eyes popped open wide.

"We know it's yours," Tabitha said. "We found it in the garbage can outside your house. It's the same shoe that left the footprint in Mr. Snipe's cement."

"I bet you put that shoe in my garbage can to make me look guilty," Fred said.

"We did not!" Tabitha cried.

"Look," said Timothy, pointing to Fred's feet. "Your shoes don't match."

"That's because I was in a rush getting dressed this morning," said Fred. "I put on the wrong shoe."

"Or maybe it's because you threw away one shoe," Tabitha said. "This shoe."

"Your left shoe is a perfect match to the cement shoe!" Timothy exclaimed.

Fred laughed nervously. "What if it is," he said. "But how come there's only one footprint in the cement? Answer that!"

"That's simple," Tabitha said. "You pushed your stick through this hole in the back of your shoe and reached over the cement…"

"and made the print with the shoe at the end of the stick," Timothy said. "Very clever, Fred."

Fred laughed. "A stroke of genius," he said, boasting. "Mr. Snipe never would have figured it out. Too bad you found that shoe."

Fred shrugged his shoulders and wandered off down the street.

Mr. Snipe Learns the Truth

Timothy and Tabitha swallowed hard
and rang Mr. Snipe's doorbell.
"You two!" Mr. Snipe exclaimed.

The twins explained to Mr. Snipe how they discovered that Fred was the one who left the print.

Mr. Snipe's jaw dropped two notches.

"That's good detective work," he said admiringly. "And now let's see what happens when I speak to the Klotches about their son!"

Mr. Snipe dashed off down the street in the direction of Fred's house.

A few days later, Tabitha and Timothy were examining the new square of wet cement in front of Mr. Snipe's house.

Clarabel stretched a paw over the cement.

"No, Clarabel!" Tabitha cried. "Don't touch the cement."

Clarabel meowed and ran up a tree.

"We'd better play catch down the street," Tabitha said.

"Yeah," said Timothy. "From now on, Mr. Snipe will have to look after his wet cement…"

"all by himself!" Tabitha said.